First published by Parragon in 2013
Parragon
Chartist House
15–17 Trim Street
Bath BA1 1HA, UK
www.parragon.com

Written by David Bedford
Illustrated by Brenna Vaughan and Henry St Leger
Edited by Laura Baker
Designed by Ailsa Cullen
Production by Rob Simenton

ISBN 978-1-4723-0301-1
Printed in China

I love my Grandpa

PaRragon

Bath • New York • Singapore • Hong Kong • Cologne • Delhi
Melbourne • Amsterdam • Johannesburg • Shenzhen

One warm and sunny afternoon, Little Bear went for a walk by the river with Grandpa Bear.

"Shall we have a paddle, Little Bear?"

Little Bear shook his head.
"I don't like water, Grandpa," he said.
"Let's just put one paw in," said Grandpa, "and see what it feels like."

Grandpa Bear put one
paw in the water.
"Ah!" he said.
"That feels good!"

Little Bear put only the tip of his paw in. Then he giggled. **"The water tickles!"** he said, and he put the rest of his paw in and waved it about.

"Wheeee!"

Grandpa Bear put
two paws in.

So did Little Bear.

Then Little Bear put all four of his little paws into the cool water.

"Well done, Little Bear!" said Grandpa.

"You're paddling! Now, are you ready to make a splash?"

Little Bear kicked his feet,
making splashes with a

swoosh-swoosh-swoosh-swoosh!

swoosh-swoosh-swoosh!

Then suddenly…

Sploosh!

In jumped Grandpa Bear,
making a gigantic splash!

"Yippee!" cried Little Bear.

"Shall we have a swim now, Little Bear?"
said Grandpa.

Little Bear shook his head.
"I can't swim, Grandpa!" he said.

"Let's just float," said Grandpa,
"and see what it feels like. I will hold you."

When Little Bear felt his grandpa holding him,
he lifted up one paw at a time, until...

"You're floating!"
said Grandpa Bear.
"Now, how about some more splashing?"

Little Bear kicked his feet, making more

swoosh-swooshes!

And suddenly...

"You're swimming,

Little Bear!" said Grandpa.

"Swim, Little Bear, swim!"

Little Bear swam around
and around his grandpa.

"You're the best little swimmer there is,"
said Grandpa Bear proudly.

When it was time to get out, Grandpa Bear helped Little Bear climb out of the water.

Then they both **wriggled** and **jiggled**
to get dry, spraying water all about.
"We're making a rainbow!" giggled Little Bear.

Grandpa Bear gave Little Bear
a warming hug.
"Do you like water now, Little
Bear?" he said, smiling.

Little Bear grinned. "I love water!"
he shouted happily. "And…"

"I love my grandpa!"